printed in the USA
ISBN 978-1-7345996-0-2

fundaments represents the first
published work by me myself,

antonio giovanni rivera

young artist, trained architect
and mixed-medium designer.

This book includes nine poems I've
written over a period of five years. Some
reminisce over the complications and joys
of relationships, others ponder about the
curiosities of growing up with eccentric
thoughts and behaviors.

Although each of the pieces was written
independently in time and train of thought,
I found common themes emerging. These
pieces have been written with attention to
spoken word and verbal expression. Each
poem has been developed for silent reading,
but more importantly vocal expression.
To be performed out loud.

Certain entries are more narrative in na-
ture. Involving abstract characters or
modulating concepts that travel forth and
back. Others follow dialogues between
counter points of thought and discussion...

We thank you kindly for deciding to join us
here, and invite you to enjoy what is within
these pages.

fundaments

poems and early writings

antonio giovanni rivera

brooklyn
new york

winter
twenty-twenty

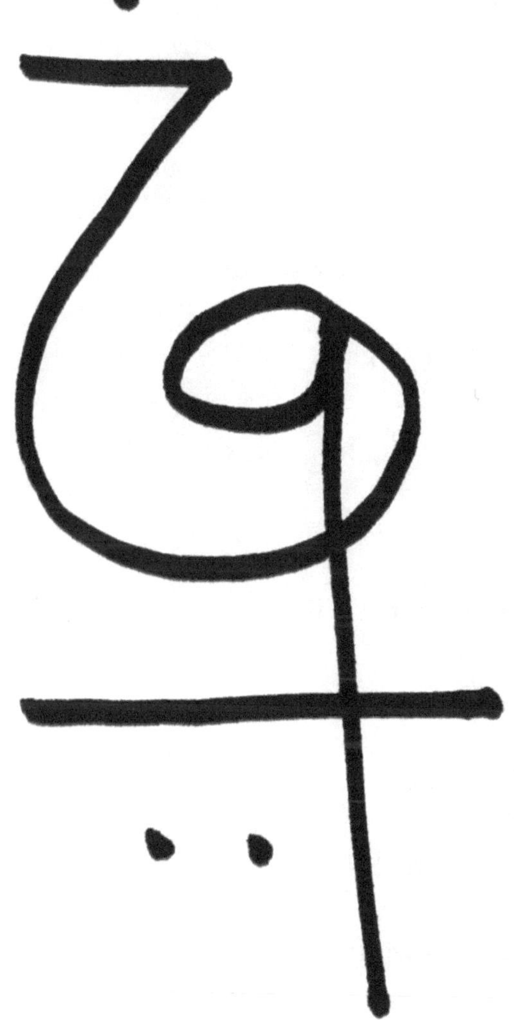

this book is dedicated to everyone
and everything that has helped
inform and guide my life up until
this point, and forever on...

included pieces

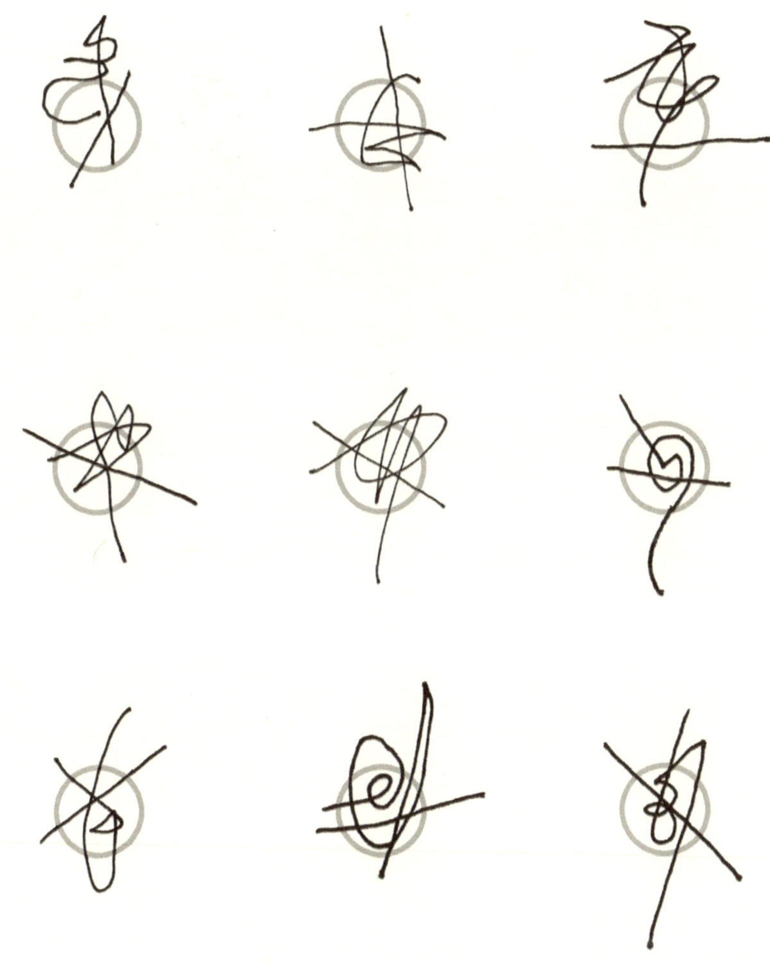

One Tree Bearing One Fruit

autumn | twenty-seventeen

One ant cannot make a colony...
Spawning fish do not lay only one egg...
No flower has but one petal.

Yet I have seen a tree once,
Which only bore a single fruit...

With groups, comes comfort and relatability.
Security is formed in numbers,
Assistance takes atleast two...

Yet I once saw upon a lonely mountaintop a lonely tree.
The very last of its kind; or perhaps just a rare breed in
these parts.

I asked the Tree,
   " Do you ever feel isolated ...

It responded,
   " I have my leafs, branches, and roots... How
     can I become alone...

I asked the tree,
    " Do you feel vulnerable; so obviously out in the
    open like this ...

It responded,
    " I have the Mountain, and can see anything
    that approaches far before its arrival ...

At this point I was quite perplexed by the tree.
Since it was receptive to my questions,
which it is said to normally not be,
I proceeded with my inquiries.

    " Are you aware of the forest beyond the Ridge there.
    I have seen many trees of numerous variety and
    quality. Would you not exist better amongst
    them there ...

    " Long ago I tried communicating with the trees
    you speak of. We found no common ground,
    could barely speak the same language.

    " If not from others of your kind, nor groups near by,
    who has taught you ...

    " The seldom passing bird has taught me much
    of the Sky, the Mountain has informed me of
    all things regarding the Ground. What lies between,
    I have learned by listening to my internal voices ...

" I have only one more question if you would
  kindly entertain me …

A breeze picked up from the Mountain's base and rustled
the Tree's leaves.

" Why do you produce only one fruit. Are you not
  worried it will be destroyed by the environment;
  worried it will not succeed in blooming …

" I am not. For I am the first and last of my
  entire kind. Failure for us is not a possibility.
  We do not feed upon the environment and elements
  that your eyes behold… We grow on a substance
  more invisible and eternal

The lonely tree spoke to me as I departed the lonely moun-
taintop and said to me:

" When the moment comes I will transfer my existence
  into the seed of this fruit, as there is no division
  between it and I. This is how I came into being
  as well..

Ground, Air, & Light

winter | twenty-seventen

In the early pre-dawn of this realm, we met in solitude to discuss our next actions. In a little while much progress had been accomplished in construction, methods, and projected variables. In short, we moved into the final stages of bringing the realm fully online.

At this moment we were seven in total. Upon completion of construction and shortly after the inaugural sunrise, four departed. Because this was an exotic build, a uniquely designed and formatted realm, new techniques were required on all fronts. The remaining three decided to combine their essences together, and supply the Realm with its Principle Code. In short, we became the Realm itself, until such point it began producing its own Code.

And there we waited.

The early beings wore little clothing, spoke little, travelled in familiar territory. Groups were formed into tribes and roles of activity seemed to come naturally. Existence for these beings had a crude simplicity to it. Battles occurred over territories or for sport.

Deep in the ground we listened to the tribal calls,
and there we waited.

The beings became more refined with much effort and
thought. Certain groups developed annual, or monthly
activities; rituals and traditions. Clothing and accessories
complimented the traditional cuisine and architecture.
Here we also saw the rise of singular rulers; chiefs, kings,
and emperors.

A few small groups were now contributing to the Realm's
Principle Code, but still we waited.

At a certain point, these scattered beings began interacting
with unfamiliar groups; no longer restricted by distance as
a result of the arrival of transportation machines.
The interactions seemed beneficial at first, but soon led to
crippling wars and demoralizing conquests. Singular
leaders reigned supreme now, and things began to look
grim for the Principle Code. The young civilizations that had
been initially contributing had left the realm at large, or
dispersed themselves amongst the others.

Softly in the air we watched the dances of force, and
there we waited.

It was now long past our anticipated arrival of the
Native Principle Code. The beings were in disarray.
No group could find unity or common ground with the
others. Traditions and conquests pit family against family,
and stranger against stranger. We introduced more

advanced technology, wiser schools of thought and activities. All of which became manipulated and perverted to suite destruction and power; not unity, not principles.

An investigation ensued in which to our great surprise we found a series of self-reproducing, cognizant and malicious codes. It was actually the inverse of what we had been waiting for. This code corrupted the Realm's infrastructure and undoubtedly its beings.

The Realm could no longer wait. We divided ourselves once more into individual essences, chose bodies, and incarnated as ourselves into ourselves. The code must be generated, and there is nothing that can stop it.

In the light we knew the way, and there we acted.

Love Letter to Terra

autumn | twenty-fifteen

We've been dancing about for a while, but I am just now
getting to see your face.
What was I seeing before this.
There, seemed to be nothing else, but now
    My gaze is fixed.

I shall tell you what I see.
In hopes of detaching from these future memories.

In your brow,
I see the angst of one thousand nations.
Torn moon-after-moon.
    Diverging from one another.

Like a well-tailored jacket, slowly ripping apart. But, unlike
the jacket, they do not de-thread at the seams. They have
been separated through invisible lines. Separated only by
the thought of their own separation in most parts.

The angst and confusion of one thousand nations.
Severed from one another,

yet stacked as a pile of loose cloth.
Touching, still unified.
    But by association, no longer thread.

In your ears,
I see the warmth of a wise woman.
Sitting or standing there.
    Still but not inert. Quiet but not silent.

Because she is absorbing the fears and worries of the
people around her.

The people who've traveled great lengths, just to be
around her. Travel, that they may cleanse themselves in her
radiance. That they may release what has grown foul
within themselves.

The warmth of a wise giving woman,
who speaks an inaudible language.
    Which all know, but few hear.

In your nose,
I see the deterioration of a robust system.
A system rich in context and complexity,
but lacking in support.
    Polluted by the negligence of so many visitors.

Similar to a garden,
which has been finely prepared and assembled,
but where no farmers arrived.

Only visitors, who took; which is no harm in itself,
but who gave not in return.

Through many rains the garden shifted and broadcasted
warnings with slight response.

Warnings which only other farmers
from other gardens heard,
     heeding the call reluctantly.

The escalating deterioration of a system
contaminated with desire,
with complacency, with ego.

But, unlike the garden, these admixtures and their patrons
are only images, mirages of actuality, preparing for
evaporation.

In your cheeks,
I see the tenacity of three craftsmen.
Swiftly moving through a brisk snow.

Craftsmen who have dedicated all extensions of their
existence to engage with and render: beauty, resolution,
design.. Extended like a flag upon its pole, with no desire to
remain near common ground, or in sight. With no desire to
demonstrate its own value or journey.

But merely converse with the wind,
and relay its principles and directions
to those watchers below.

Deep in isolation they seem,
because like miners they plunge into the soul.
Removed. Out of mind.
    Yet return with gold.

The productivity of three tenacious craftsmen,
who are now conquering obstacles, simplifying enigmas.
Pollinating thought.

Their only request
is to continue on their quest;
one of self-knowledge.

They only suggest,
that of the richness and
beneficence they've found,
we digest.

In your mouth,
I see the incompetence of a lonely observer.
Searching without reward
through empty promises
    passed down through generations.

Promises and thoughts which are completely hollow from
the inside looking outward, yet bright and enticing from
the outside.

Lying on their back,
with historical hopes running through their eyes.
Alone, confused.
Because they have been convinced so.

Convinced they must search outside of themselves for
knowledge. When the things that must truly be found, only
reside inside.

The vapid incompetence
of an observer who is unable to penetrate
with their vision the core,
       where the genuine sap dwells.

And must only be satisfied
with sparse scraps of exterior bark.

In your eyes I see nothing.
I only feel.
Feel the power and depth of an advance being
       unaware of its own complexity.

Unaware of its own potential..
-No.

Aware of the potential, but only in dreams.
Only in drifting fragments of imagination.
Not yet connected or unificd.

Drifting pieces, currently realizing
the concentric cords and links to infinity they posses.

I feel the depth, through your eyes still,
slowly encompassing my presence.
Slowly forming an impression upon my ruling principle.

Perhaps this is how you ensnared me in the first place.
How you coaxed me into this dance, into this

delicate exchange of force. I cannot say if I am satisfied or
not. I can only continue dancing.
  Continue revealing what I see.. What I feel.

The power I feel resides not directly
in your eyes, but very near.
Lies in your persistence and dedication.
Continually pushing and thrusting yourself
toward something not possible to grasp completely.

Something that lies waiting in your deepest roots, lies wait-
ing directly above your crown. Although your success is
eminent. Is already completely unfolded before you.
  It remains a mystery. Still enveloped in its own
  morning fog.

An advanced being who is complete and entire.
Who can expand and unfold without losing its
original image.

Soon, we will finish dancing.
But in my mind this cannot end.
Because I have now been introduced to so many things.

Your scent will linger throughout my sensations for...

Those Who Shall

summer | twenty-sixteen

Let those who shall,
    come.

For the burden of proof will be
their water bucket to carry,
    their task to achieve and overcome.

But let not them be in haste,
or with desire in heart and eyes.

For here,
no such player can move forward.
No such engagement or parlay
unfolds within our confines.

Let not those afraid of
outcomes or self-revealings
show their faces.

For here we are built on top of stones,
    and beneath the sky.

We are built rigid and compacted,
yet flexible when need be.
Atleast now we are,
    and say nothing of the past.

When you are near, it becomes visible.
If you are inside, it becomes tangible.
And if you are,
    then so are we.

We have felt the pressure of
one thousand realities,
combined into singularity.
The pressure of a
    genuinely thick density.

And those who come must be
strong but enduring, wise but agile.
They must be prepared to move
the blocks of progression into place,
    and stride through undetermined footprints.

And those who will not succeed
are many.
And those who will have tried their hardest
are every.

For here, there is not one counted amongst them all,
    who was not aware of the tasks before hand;
    was not pre-emptively engaged and debriefed.

The risk was high, but the rewards higher.
The sweetest sap in all
the discovered realms lies undisturbed
    at the core of a rock-like trunk.

Lies waiting for the moment the light rays
will touch its naked body.
The moment it will slowly fall,
    sweetly,

but slowly fall into the digestion
of the Eternal Beings.

Let those too weak or
easily disturbed remain outside.
Remain watching from a distance
as we bud our first flower,
    and shoot our first branches.

We are here.
We have always been here,
in altered forms.
    but speak nothing of the future.

Let those who shall,
come.

Because the tipping point
has been obtained,
The Cartographers have
regained their maps and keys.

You watching,
has there,
will be anything of equal caliber,
    of equal nutrients.

If so,
remain watching.
For here,
    It will all be satisfied...

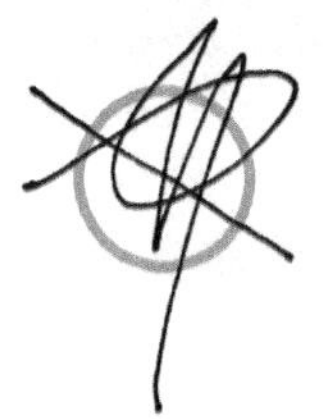

A Banana Shaped Life

summer | twenty-sixteen

Reclined from the general tendencies of most,
you will find me directly aside the rhythm,
or forced cadence as I see it,
of social normalities...
    Banalities?

Perhaps they are amounting to a sum,
providing a feature, or equating to some total...
But I cannot see it.

Removed I have,
like a winged painting from its chrysalis,
myself from the entire affair...
    Without care?

Separation was birthed and nurtured
by internal tides and freedom song.
Division had not bee an agenda,
but natural course of action...
    Extraction?

There is a risk involved in isolation.
No common ground stunts communication.
and stagnant solitude breeds perturbation.
     But yet, no other way has come to stay.

The groove of tenacity can easily become a canyon,
with walls terminating only at perspective's end.

However, just as easily,
it can become the bed for a nourishing river,
terminating only at rich delta's head.

Started a drawing once, ontop skin of left hand.
The influence provided by the existing
lines and crevices was tremendous.
Had known better, would have stopped trying to
defeat the grain from onset.

Once harmonious lines from ink and dermis appeared,
was no longer drawing,
but revealing...

And so this outcast life unfolds in like manner.
It is perhaps living itself, and I just the motor.
The existence-grade fuel it needs to become resolute,
     in order.

To become something it is not already,
or atleast become more of what it is.
     The difference deceives me.

And so finding others on similar trajectory
becomes a burdensome task,
     again the risk of isolation.

Yet all are too busy and light,
like white painting flapping obscurely
from one flower to the next.

From open fields to closed bulbs.
There is dimly a chance to connect, engage,
     or make love.

Is the disk exhausted from
constant outpouring of light...
Does she ask for respite or relief...

Then I shall act in similar fashion,
until some moon offers alternative course.
And even then,
     I will only half exhaust my efforts.

Tried a normal existence once.
Following this or that suggestion
as supported by high usage.
Saw things only how they appear to be,
with no interest in how they are.

Worse advice I ever received:
     " Stop being so weird.

Weird meant in past:
     " One who controls their destiny.

The responsibility involved blinds most,
depletes others,
     and forgets the rest.

But if you shall have none of this,
I fear you will only be left with a banana shaped candy,
painted yellow and injected with substitute
banana flavoring...

The genuine sap is as difficult
as it has to be,
to protect itself from unworthy tasters
trying to set it free...

Without Exception

summer | twenty-seventeen

Is the tree delusional of its destiny to bear fruit.
Does the river refuse the inevitability
of joining the ocean, someday.

Has not the caterpillar some inkling of its
destiny to metamorph into a winged painting.
From a slow-moving, gravity-bound line,
into a roaming and care-free butter flyer.

Then why does man grieve himself
over his true purpose,
to receive Death and Liberation.
For death is no end...

Yes, you must continue elsewhere,
but of how many other realms and
possibilities you have, we cannot catalogue.

Even when you promised to live,
you agreed to die.
Agreed to remove the goggles of existence
eventually, and not leave,
but return to your larger abode.

Let us work in reverse:
Death is Life.
They are simply the same body
viewed from opposing angles.

Or to extend this reversion:
Life is only a prelude to True Life,
where we are actually dead now.
Atleast in a dead, un-live state.
Perhaps a form of preparation.
A form of cultivation for
the experience of True Life.

What if True Life really began once we died.
We are the dead, and the embrace of Death
delivers us onto Life.

However, there is much to accomplish
here and now.
True Life and Life are not better or worse
than each other, Because again,
we are already truely living, only wearing goggles.

Now here, we must continue to progress.
Continue to learn and teach,
continue because there is no alternative.

To wait?
Do you think this is even possible...

I have seen them try,
and can assure you not one succeeded.

I have seen waiting so intense,
it turned into change accidentally.

For progress is beyond the control
of Livers and Dyers.
They can only postpone or anticipate it.

To work with it, seems best.
Working against will only increase
the velocity of upgrades,
when their moment blossoms.

Because there is no reality
in which they shall not blossom,
shall not deluge, progress.

If you do indeed contribute to Life,
are a companion of beautiful upgrades,
then there is a great Death in store for you.
If you are against, you will be converted with no exceptions.

Then a great Life, and
a great Death shall be yours as well.

Eye of My Edge

spring | twenty-fifteen

And so the two were off...
They gently strolled near the trees and through the bushes.
   Life never seemed more real to them than now.

And when it was time for dinner,
   who cared.
The food would remain, the fire would be available.
But right now, they were off.

It didn't matter that the one had a hard time staying asleep.
It didn't matter that the other couldn't tell any lies.

The one could only ride bicycles with low seats.
The one could only yell loudly, if it was an emergency.

The one had something to say, but never accepted there
might be an appropriate moment to do so.
The one would rather speak, only with eyes and eyebrows.
And give small gestures with pinky fingers.

The trees stopped.
The birds all flew away singing their travelling songs...
And there they were.
    They were no longer off.

They stood for many instances in this state of absence.
    Then sat for a few more.

I don't know why I do all the things I do... But I know
I should be doing them,
    said the one.
Then how do you know they are the right things.. A bird
could chirp, and change your mind
    said the one,

But birds have no business chirping to me.
It will only get lost in the soothing breeze of now...
I feel like I'm not here... maybe that has something to do
about it.
    said the one.

If that's so, then where could you be,
    said the one
It's not the same. I don't have to always be somewhere,
    said the one.

One of them has had a hard time relating ideas to people.
It didn't matter that the other could discuss on end, and ar-
rive in a nice garden.

By now, the grass had also stopped.
The wind was down, and the clouds were high.
	Dinner was so far away now, it seemed like lunch.
But they wanted to go further,
	and so they did.

	And so the two were off.
This instance surrounded by shades of deep blue
and indigo. They eagerly lunged near the oranges, and
through the yellows.

Life never seemed more like Life to them now,
And it didn't matter if it was real or not.

One spoke, but only emitted the word
	dark crimson.
One responded with a soft whisper of,
	misty green.

The two looked at each other intently for a while.
They knew they would never meet again.
They knew they could meet again later, but it would have
been greatly past dinner,
	and the soothing ripeness of now will have been spoiled.

The one knew things.
The one wanted to know more, but didn't know how
to introduce.
The one felt this and said:

I can't keep to myself. [translated]

I've known you for too long. [translated]

Sometimes, people don't know themselves. [translated]

You act like someone stuck in a novel. [translated]

I can't stop thinking if people use to be. [translated]

What would it change...

At this, the one who didn't ask the question became
very silent.
The hurricane of shades, tonal values, and ideals became
unstable.
    It shifted in many gyrations of discord.

The one had no answer, nor proceeding question,
    only a statement:
The clouds look very round
From so far down....

Nice Guys Finish Last

summer | twenty-nineteen

They say nice guys finish last..
And it's true! The other night
I was enjoying the company of a woman,
enjoying her curls, conversations, and kisses.

And you know what... I finished last.
That's right... When you're a nice guy you value
putting others before yourself.
Help them reveal their wealth.

If you want to finish first,

then others you might have to hurt.
You'll have to put a few people in the dirt,
put them down until they don't know their worth,

then you can easily finish first.

They say the early bird gets the worm...
But the second mouse gets the cheese...

And you know, I like to finish last.
So I can capitalize off the
mistakes and failures of the past.

Develop myself and map out my own path.
I'm not in a race with these other cats.

I'd rather fly up above, like the hawk,
with every path at my disposal.

When advice I need, with the trees I'll talk,
of keeping quality and substance as my proposal.

Slowly,
and forever on.

Leading, Following

summer | twenty-eighteen

Clouds billowing, bustling, bubbling.
Decisions, reactions,
happenings, passings

A beam of light through
the dark thick density.
Birds gone, stars gone,
further vision prolonged.

Until the rain came.

Drenching myself in decisions
was the only way to maintain...

Stay in the proper lane,
while moving through the game...
Keep my head straight,
while moving through the game...

We are moving,
through the game.

When a thing happens,
another one follows.
But we must monitor if these things
are full or hollow.

Had a dream once, knew reality.
Had a life twice, knew illusion.
Failed all three times,
just to learn the fuckin' difference...

And I followed the vine,
all the way to the root.
Followed ant crawling on ground,
all the way to the fruit.

Lead the way,
from sun, to ray, to leaf.
Lead the way,
from cool shadow, to heat.

Still couldn't tell you
which came first...

www.ingramcontent.com/pod-product-compliance
Lightning Source LLC
Chambersburg PA
CBHW021206110726
47900CB00002B/759